Quinito's Neighborhood

El vecindario de Quinito

Story / Cuento
Ina Cumpiano

Illustrations / Ilustraciones
José Ramírez

Children's Book Press / Editorial Libros para Niños

My mami is a carpenter.
My papi is a nurse.

Mi mami es carpintera.
Mi papi es enfermero.

My abuela drives a big truck.
My abuelo fixes clocks.

Sometimes my abuela
brings broken grandfather clocks
to my abuelo's shop.

Mi abuela maneja
un camión bien grande.
Mi abuelo es relojero.

A veces mi abuela
lleva relojes de caja
que no funcionan
al taller de mi abuelo.

5

My tía is a muralist.
My tío teaches dance.

Mi tía es muralista.
Mi tío da clases de baile.

My grown-up cousin Tita goes to clown school.

Mi prima Tita, que ya es grande, va a la escuela para ser payasa.

Her brother,
my primo Ruperto, is a dentist.
He checks people's teeth.

Su hermano,
mi primo Ruperto, es dentista.
Le examina los dientes
a la gente.

My neighbors,
Rafi and Luis Manuel,
go to work very early.
Rafi bakes bread
and Luis Manuel sells it.

Mis vecinos,
Rafi y Luis Manuel,
salen a trabajar
muy tempranito.

Rafi hace el pan
y Luis Manuel lo vende.

12

Mrs. Hernández sells Rafi's bread at her bodega, too.

And her daughter, Sonia Isabel, counts the money in the bank on the corner.

La señora Hernández también vende
el pan de Rafi en su bodega.

Y su hija, Sonia Isabel, cuenta dinero
en el banco de la esquina.

Guillermo is our mailman.
Guillermo is going to marry
Sonia Isabel.

Guillermo es cartero.
Guillermo se va a casar
con Sonia Isabel.

17

Doña Estrella is a seamstress.
She is sewing a wedding dress
for Sonia Isabel.

Doña Estrella es costurera.
Le está cosiendo el traje de boda
a Sonia Isabel.

Mr. Gómez
is Doña Estrella's neighbor.
He is also my teacher at school.

Mrs. Gómez is a crossing guard.
She helps me cross the street.

El señor Gómez
es el vecino de Doña Estrella.
También es mi maestro.

La señora Gómez es la guardia escolar.
Me ayuda a cruzar la calle.

And I am a very busy person, too.
I have to tell Mr. Gómez
that my mami is a carpenter
and my papi is a nurse.

Y yo, también, soy una persona muy ocupada.
Le tengo que decir al señor Gómez
que mi mami es carpintera
y mi papi es enfermero.

the writer and the artist

Ina Cumpiano

Ina Cumpiano is a Puerto Rican poet and translator who now lives in a busy, friendly neighborhood in San Francisco, California. As a teenager, she was a television actress, and she has since worked as a cashier, a teacher of languages and literature, and a free-lance writer and editor. She has published nearly twenty books for children. But her favorite job so far has been as a grandmother: she has ten grandchildren, ages two to thirteen.

For my five—Maya, Benjamin, Leah, Devin, and Kaitlyn, and for the five that are as good as mine—Jordan, Annabelle, Austin, Ezra, and Hugo. / *Para mis cinco—Maya, Benjamin, Leah, Devin y Kaitlyn, y para los cinco que son casi míos— Jordan, Annabelle, Austin, Ezra y Hugo.* —I.C.

José Ramírez

José Ramírez was born in Los Angeles, California. He is a gifted artist and also a second grade teacher for the Los Angeles Unified School District. His paintings, ceramic sculptures, and tile murals have been shown in museums, galleries, bookstores, coffee shops, and public spaces in the US and abroad. He has also conducted art workshops for museums, various community-based organizations, musician's groups, and after-school programs in and around Los Angeles, where he lives. This is his fourth book for children.

I dedicate this book to all the students I've taught and learned from over the past twelve years. / *Dedico este libro a todos los estudiantes que he enseñado y de los cuales he aprendido durante los últimos doce años.* —J.R.

words to know

abuelo - grandfather
abuela - grandmother
tío - uncle
tía - aunt
primo - male cousin
prima - female cousin
bodega - small neighborhood grocery store

Story copyright © 2005 by Children's Book Press
Illustrations copyright © 2005 by José Ramírez

These illustrations were done in acrylic on canvas. The fonts are Child's Play, Providence Sans, and ITC Stone Serif.

Editor: Dana Goldberg
Design and Art Direction: Carl Angel

Special thanks to Laura Chastain, Rosalyn Sheff, and the staff of Children's Book Press.

Children's Book Press

is a nonprofit publisher of multicultural and bilingual literature for children. Write to us for a complimentary catalog:
Children's Book Press, 2211 Mission St, San Francisco, CA 94110.
Visit us on the Internet:
www.childrensbookpress.org

An activity guide is available for this book on our website.

Printed in Singapore through Tien Wah Press
10 9 8 7 6 5 4 3 2 1

Distributed to the book trade by Publishers Group Wes[t]
Quantity discounts available through the publisher for educational and nonprofit use.

Library of Congress Cataloging-in-Publication Data
Cumpiano, Ina.
Quinito's Neighborhood = El Vecindario de Quinito / b[y]
Ina Cumpiano; illustrations by José Ramírez.
p. cm.
Summary: Quinito not only knows everyone in his neighborhood, he also knows that each person in his community has a different, important occupation.
ISBN 0-89239-209-6
I. Title: El vecindario de Quinito. II. Ramírez, José.
III. Title.
PZ73.C86 2005
2004065506